MAX AND DIANA AND THE
SHOPPING TRIP

by Harriet Ziefert

Drawings by Lonni Sue Johnson

Harper & Row, Publishers

I'm Diana.
My twin brother's name is Max.
Today our Daddy is taking us on errands.
"Race you to the car!" Max says.

We get there at the same time.
I sit on one side of the back seat
and Max sits on the other.
Daddy makes sure we buckle
our seat belts.
Vroom! Vroom!
The car starts.
We're off!

"Here we are," says Daddy.
Max runs ahead to the barbershop.
He gets there first.

But I get the first haircut.
Snip! Snip!
Max has to wait his turn.

Daddy tells the barber
how to cut my brother's hair.
Max won't sit still.
He keeps looking around
to see what I'm doing.

We walk to the shoe store.
Max wants to look in windows.

Daddy wants to get there fast.
"Hurry up!" he says.

When we get there,
a man measures my feet.
Max yells, "She always goes first!"

Daddy asks the man to measure Max's feet.
He says, "Your feet and her feet are exactly
the same size. You must be twins!"

"I can bring you white sneakers
or purple ones," the man says.
"I want purple," Max answers.

Max likes the purple sneakers.
He doesn't want to take them off.
Not ever.

"What color sneakers do you want?"
the man asks me.
"I want white — with red stripes!"
The shoe store man finds sneakers for me.

Daddy says Max and I can wear
our new sneakers home.
Daddy pays.
The cashier gives us balloons.

Daddy ties Max's balloon around his wrist.
Then he ties mine.

"Let's run," says Max.
     We run faster and faster and faster.

Max's balloon flies up in the air.
He starts to cry. "Daddy, you
don't know how to tie knots."

Daddy says he's sorry the balloon blew away. Then he says, "I'm going to buy you something that will last a long time."

Daddy takes us to the bookstore.
It's our favorite place.

Daddy lets Max choose a book.
And he lets me choose one too.

Two books.
One for Max.
One for Diana.
Happy reading!